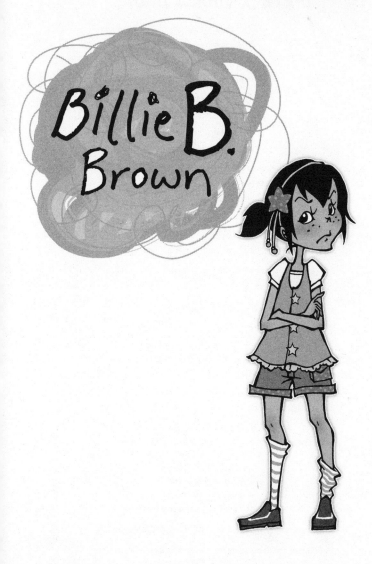

Billie B. Brown

www.BillieBBrownBooks.com

Billie B. Brown Books

First American Edition 2015
Kane Miller, A Division of EDC Publishing

Text copyright © 2012 Sally Rippin
Illustrations copyright © 2012 Aki Fukuoka
First published in Australia in 2012 by Hardie Grant Egmont

For information contact:
Kane Miller, A Division of EDC Publishing
P.O. Box 470663
Tulsa, OK 74147-0663
www.kanemiller.com
www.edcpub.com
www.usbornebooksandmore.com

Library of Congress Control Number: 2014950302

Printed and bound in the United States of America
3 4 5 6 7 8 9 10

ISBN: 978-1-61067-389-1

Billie B. Brown

The Copycat Kid

By Sally Rippin

Illustrated by Aki Fukuoka

Kane Miller
A DIVISION OF EDC PUBLISHING

Chapter One

Billie B. Brown has one fancy headband, two purple shoes and three star buttons on her top. Do you know what the "B" in Billie B. Brown stands for?

Buddy.

There is a new girl arriving in Billie's class today. Her name is Mika. She has come all the way from Japan.

Ms. Walton has asked Billie to be Mika's buddy. She can't wait. She has dressed up especially. Doesn't she look nice?

One fancy headband

Three star buttons

Two purple shoes

Billie and her best friend, Jack, walk to school with his mom. They are very **excited** to meet Mika.

"I wonder what she'll be like?" Billie says. "Ms. Walton says she has black hair like me"

Billie and Jack reach the school gate.

Ella and Tracey are waiting for them.

"Cool top!" says Tracey.

"Thanks," says Billie. "I just got it this weekend."

"The new girl is here!" Ella says. "Come and see. She's in the classroom."

Billie and Jack run after Ella and Tracey.

They all peer in the
classroom window.
Ms. Walton is talking
to the new girl's mom.
The new girl has black
hair and big brown eyes.

Billie thinks she looks
lovely.

Ms. Walton sees them
peeking through the
window. "Billie, come
and meet Mika," she calls.

Ella and Tracey run
over to the monkey bars.
Jack goes to play soccer.
Billie walks into the
classroom to meet Mika.

"Mika, this is Billie," says
Ms. Walton. "She will
look after you until you
know your way around."

"Hi!" says Billie excitedly.
"Nice to meet you!"

Mika looks at Billie.
Then she looks at her mom.
Mika's mom smiles and
says something to Mika
in Japanese. Mika nods
and her cheeks turn pink.
"Hello," she says quietly.

"Mika doesn't speak much English yet," Ms. Walton explains to Billie.

"Oh," says Billie.

Just then the bell **rings**. All the kids in Billie's class start coming inside and sitting at their desks.

Normally Billie sits next to Jack, but today she sits with Mika.

Jack waves at her
from their usual seat.
Billie waves back.
She feels very **proud**.
She is a good buddy!

Chapter Two

At recess, Billie and Mika
sit under the big tree. They
eat their snacks and watch
the kids in the playground.
Billie smiles at Mika.
Mika smiles back.

All day long Billie looks
after Mika. Sometimes
Billie does actions to
explain to Mika what
Ms. Walton is saying.
But mostly Mika just
watches what Billie does.

Billie is sure that
Ms. Walton will be
very happy with her.

The next morning
Billie gets ready quickly.
Then she waits at her
front door for Jack. She is
excited to see Mika again.

When they get to school,

Billie rushes straight into the classroom to look for Mika.

"Hi, Billie," says Ms. Walton. "Mika will be happy to see you. In fact, it looks like you have a fan!"

Billie looks over to where Mika is sitting. Mika stands up and waves to Billie.

Then she turns around
in a circle to show Billie
what she has on.
Billie can't believe her
eyes! Mika is wearing…

One fancy headband, two
purple shoes and three
star buttons on her top.

Just like Billie was
wearing yesterday!

Billie *is* surprised. She feels **strange** seeing Mika wearing the same clothes as her. Billie likes looking different. She doesn't know what to say.

But Mika just smiles and follows Billie out into the playground.

Lola is standing over at the water fountain with Tracey and Ella. Billie likes Tracey and Ella, but Lola can be annoying.

"Hey," Tracey says. "Mika has the same top as Billie."

"They must be twins!"
Lola says.

Billie feels her face
get hot. "No, we're not!"
she says. "That's just silly."

But secretly she feels **cross**
that Mika has copied her.

Chapter Three

At recess, Mika follows

Billie to the soccer field.

They sit down to watch.

Jack runs up to them.

"Hi, Billie," he says. "Do you

want to join our team?"

"Um…" Billie isn't sure. She loves playing soccer, but she doesn't want to leave Mika on her own.

"Come on," pleads Jack. "We're losing. We need you!"

"Oh, all right," says Billie. Then she turns to Mika. "You wait here. OK?" She taps the bench. "I am going to play soccer." Billie points to the soccer field.

Mika smiles and nods. Then, before Billie can say anything, Mika runs onto the soccer field! Billie's mouth drops open.

What? That's not
what Billie meant!
She watches Mika run
after the ball. Mika is fast.
Very fast! Maybe even
faster than Billie.

"Hey, Mika is good at soccer!" Jack says. Then he runs onto the field too.

Billie plonks back down on the bench and squeezes her mouth tight. She feels a big **angry** ball growing inside her. It's not fair! Billie is the best girl at soccer. Not Mika!

When the bell rings,
Billie stomps back to class.
Mika follows her.

The next lesson is art.

Mika sits next to Billie.

Billie is still feeling cross.

"OK, class," says Ms. Walton.

"Today I'd like you all to draw an imaginary land. I want you all to come up with something unique."

Hmmm… thinks Billie. *Something unique.*

Then Billie has an idea. A super-duper idea. She will draw a polka-dot land. Polka-dot trees,

polka-dot houses,
even polka-dot people.

*No one else will think
of that!* thinks Billie.
She works hard on
her drawing all class.

Ms. Walton walks over.
"That's a wonderful
drawing!" she says
from behind Billie.

"Thanks!" says Billie,
feeling proud. But when
she looks up, she sees
that Ms. Walton is speaking
to Mika.

Billie looks over at Mika's
drawing and **gasps**.

Mika has drawn a polka-dot land too. Polka-dot trees, houses – even polka-dot people. Just like Billie!

Billie is **furious**. That was her idea! She feels like she is going to explode. She stands up and stomps her foot.

"Stop copying me!" she shouts at Mika.

29

Mika looks at Billie.

Her eyes grow very wide.

Just then, the bell rings
for lunch. Billie runs
out of the classroom.
She never wants to be
a buddy again!

Chapter Four

Billie sits under the big
tree in the playground.
She still feels angry.
But she also feels a
teensy bit bad for
shouting at Mika.

Billie sees Ms. Walton
walking towards her.
She feels nervous.
She is sure Ms. Walton
is going to be cross.
Ms. Walton sits down on
the bench beside Billie.

"You know you shouldn't have shouted at Mika," Ms. Walton says.

Billie nods. "I know," she says. "It's just that… it's just…she won't stop copying me. It's SO annoying!"

Ms. Walton smiles. "I said you had a fan, didn't I?"

Billie frowns. "She doesn't have to do everything I do!"

"Imagine what it must be like for Mika," says Ms. Walton. "Everything is new and different for her. Imagine if you couldn't understand what anyone was saying."

Billie thinks about this. It sounds **scary**.

34

"Then imagine if you met someone who looked after you. Someone kind, like you, Billie," says Ms. Walton.

Billie looks up at Ms. Walton in surprise.

"Mika's mom said she couldn't stop talking about you yesterday," says Ms. Walton. "She went shopping last night to get Mika the same top as yours."

"Really?" Billie says. She hadn't thought about it this way before. "So that's why she's copying me? Because she likes me?"

"That's right," says
Ms. Walton.

"I feel bad for shouting
at her," Billie says.

"Would you like to say
sorry?" Ms. Walton asks.

Billie nods. Ms. Walton
calls over Mika.

"I'm really sorry I yelled
at you," Billie says to Mika.

"So, do you still want
to be Mika's buddy?"
Ms. Walton asks.

Billie shakes her head.
"No," she says.
"Not anymore."

"Oh dear, why not?"
says Ms. Walton,
looking worried.

Billie grins at Mika.
"Because I'd rather be
your friend."

Mika looks confused.

*Maybe she doesn't
understand me*, thinks Billie.
Then she has an idea.
A super-duper idea.

"Wait here!" she says.

Billie runs to the school library. She sits down in front of a computer and types in a message. Another message comes up on the screen in strange squiggly letters. Billie copies them onto a piece of paper.

Billie can't understand
the words, but she knows
Mika will. Do you know
why? That's right! Billie
is writing in Japanese.
Can you guess what
it says? Turn over the
page for the answer.

42

Collect them all!

Billie B. Brown
The Bad Butterfly
By Sally Rippin

Billie B. Brown
The Soccer Star
By Sally Rippin

Billie B. Brown
The Midnight Feast
By Sally Rippin

Billie B. Brown
The Second-best Friend
By Sally Rippin

Billie B. Brown
The Extra-special Helper
By Sally Rippin

Billie B. Brown
The Beautiful Haircut
By Sally Rippin

Billie B. Brown
The Big Sister
By Sally Rippin

Billie B. Brown
The Spotty Vacation
By Sally Rippin

Billie B. Brown
The Birthday Mix-up
By Sally Rippin

Billie B. Brown
The Secret Message
By Sally Rippin

Billie B. Brown
The Little Lie
By Sally Rippin

Billie B. Brown
The Best Project
By Sally Rippin

Billie B. Brown
The Deep End
By Sally Rippin

Billie B. Brown
The Copycat Kid
By Sally Rippin

Billie B. Brown
The Night Fright
By Sally Rippin